Iris and Walter
and the Field Trip

Iris and Walter
and the Field Trip

WRITTEN BY

Elissa Haden Guest

ILLUSTRATED BY

Christine Davenier

sandpiper

Green Light Readers

Houghton Mifflin Harcourt

Boston   New York

To Phyllis, who makes every field trip fabulous—E.H.G.

For Josephine, my wonderful little mermaid—C.D.

Text copyright © 2005 by Elissa Haden Guest
Illustrations copyright © 2005 by Christine Davenier

SANDPIPER and the SANDPIPER logo are trademarks of
Houghton Mifflin Harcourt Publishing Company.
Green Light Readers and its logo are trademarks of Houghton Mifflin Harcourt Publishing Company,
registered in the United States of America and/or its jurisdictions.

For information about permission to reproduce selections from this book, write to Permissions,
Houghton Mifflin Harcourt Publishing Company, 215 Park Avenue South, New York, New York 10003.

www.hmhbooks.com

First Green Light Readers edition 2013

The text of this book is set in Fairfield Medium.
The display type is set in Elroy.
The illustrations were created in pen-and-ink on keacolor paper.

The Library of Congress has cataloged the hardcover edition as follows:
Guest, Elissa Haden
Iris and Walter and the field trip/written by Elissa Haden Guest; illustrated by Christine Davenier
p. cm.
Summary: When best friends Iris and Walter go on a field trip to an aquarium, Walter gets lost and a worried Iris helps Miss Cherry look for him.
[1. School field trips—Fiction. 2. Lost children—Fiction. 3. Aquariums, Public—Fiction.
4. Friendship—Fiction.]
I. Davenier, Christine, ill. II. Title. III. Series.
PZ7.G9375Iskq 2005
[E]—dc22 2003027022

ISBN: 978-0-15-205014-6 hardcover
ISBN: 978-0-544-10665-9 paperback

Manufactured in China
SCP 10 9 8 7 6 5 4 3 2 1

4500421615

Contents

1. The Aquarium!

One day, Iris's teacher, Miss Cherry,
had an exciting announcement.
"This Friday, we're going on a field trip
to the aquarium."
"The aquarium!" said Iris's best friend,
Walter. "Oh boy!"

"Are we going to see the sharks?"
asked Benny.

"Are we going to see the penguins?"
asked Iris.

"Are we going to see the starfish?"
asked Jenny.

"We are all going to see many wonderful things," said Miss Cherry.

That night, Walter had supper at Iris's house.
"Our class is going on a field trip, Rosie,"
said Iris.
"Up," said Baby Rose.

"Where are you going?" asked Iris's father.

"We're going to the aquarium," said Iris.

"On the bus!" said Walter.

"And we're going to see the penguins,"
Iris told Grandpa.
"I love penguins," said Grandpa.
"And after that, we're going to have
a picnic in the park," said Walter.

"Oh my! I wish I were going on the field trip,"
said Iris's mother.

"Hey, Walter, do you want to be bus buddies?"
Iris asked.

"Sure!" said Walter.

2. The Bus Ride

On Friday morning, Miss Cherry said,
"We are very lucky to have
Jenny's mother come on the field trip
with us today."
Jenny gave her mother a big hug.
"I know we are going to have
a great time," said Miss Cherry.

"Now let's go over the rules. Remember, pay attention. Hang on to your partner. Stay with the group. And if you get lost, stay where you are and I will find you," said Miss Cherry.

"I've never been lost, have you?"
Iris asked Lulu.

"No. And I sure wouldn't want to be,"
said Lulu.

"That would be scary," said Benny.

"Really scary," said Walter.

The children climbed aboard the school bus.

Iris and Walter chose the very last seat.

They bounced up and down.

Benny told knock-knock jokes.

Lulu made up silly fish songs.

Everyone was happy and excited.

Nobody thought any more about getting lost.

3. Where's Walter?

When the bus pulled up in
front of the aquarium, Iris said,
"Look at all the people!"
"Hey, Walter," said Benny.
"That boy is wearing a shirt
just like yours."
"He is!" said Walter.

"Now children, it's very crowded here,
so keep your eyes on me," said Miss Cherry.

The children walked down a dark hallway.
Everywhere they looked there were fish.
"Ooh," they whispered.

"Sharks!" said Benny.

"They look mean," said Iris.

While the children were looking
at the sharks, Miss Cherry
and Jenny's mother counted everyone.
"Okay, follow me," said Miss Cherry.

They came to the coral reef.

"Wow!" said Iris and Benny.

Walter could not say a word.
He watched the angelfish swim and shimmer,
the hermit crabs scurry, and the sea grass
sway. Walter had never seen anything
as wonderful as the coral reef.

"Are we going to see the penguins soon?"
asked Iris.

"That's our next stop," said Miss Cherry.
And she counted everyone again.

"Off we go," said Miss Cherry.

They walked past the starfish.

They walked past the sea horses.

"Oh, look, there are the penguins!"
said Iris, taking Walter's hand.

"Don't you think they are cute, Walter?"
But Walter didn't answer.

Iris turned around. She saw a boy.

"You're not Walter," said Iris.

"I'm Nick," said the boy.

"Where's my class?" he asked.

Iris looked all around.

There were crowds of children.

She could not see Walter anywhere.

"There you are, Nick!" shouted a woman.

"I've been looking all over for you."

Nick grabbed his teacher's hand

and held on tight.

Iris ran to Miss Cherry.

"Miss Cherry, I can't find Walter!" she said.

"Walter's lost?" asked Jenny.

"I can't find him anywhere!" said Iris.

4. The Rescue

"Don't worry," said Miss Cherry.
"I will find Walter. Now, I want everyone
to stay with Jenny's mother."
"Please let me come with you," said Iris.
Miss Cherry looked at Iris's worried face.
"Come, Iris. You and I shall find Walter,"
said Miss Cherry.

They walked past the starfish.
They did not see Walter.

They walked
by the sea horses,
but Walter was not there.

Iris thought about Walter, lost and alone.
"Poor Walter. He must be really scared,"
she said.
"We will find him," said Miss Cherry.
But there were so many people.
How would they ever find Walter
in the big crowd?

Suddenly, Iris saw him.

"There he is! There's Walter!" she cried.

Walter was still standing

in front of the coral reef,

watching the fish swim around and around.

"Walter, we've been looking
for you everywhere!" said Iris.
"Huh?" said Walter.
"I was so worried," said Iris.
"Why?" asked Walter.
"Because you were lost!" said Iris.
"I was?" he asked.

Iris and Miss Cherry gave Walter a big hug.
"I'm very happy to see you, Walter,"
said Miss Cherry. "And now, I think
it's a good time to have our picnic.
Don't you?"

Outside, the sun was shining.
Iris and Walter played tag with their friends.
They sat under a tree
and shared their lunches.
"Time to go!" said Miss Cherry.

When the bus pulled up in front of school,
Grandpa was waiting.
"How was the field trip?" he asked.

"It was fabulous," said Walter.

"We saw angelfish and hermit crabs!"

"And Walter got lost!" said Iris.

"Oh no!" said Grandpa.

"But I didn't know I was lost!" said Walter.

"And I found him," said Iris.

Then Iris and Walter told Grandpa
the whole story,
all the way home.